Chapter 1: The Note on the Bench

Some benches are just wood and rust.
Others remember everything.

I don't know why I went back to that bench.
Maybe I missed the silence.
Or maybe I was just tired of pretending the
noise didn't bother me.

The air that evening wasn't heavy with rain.
It was heavier than that.
It was the kind of quiet that made you feel
like the world had paused just to watch you
fall apart.

I pulled my hoodie over my head, same as
always. Cap underneath, eyes low.
I didn't want the world to see me.
I didn't want to see it either.

This bench...
It had watched me become someone I can't
even recognize now.

Same spot. Same lake. Same ache in my
chest that I've carried like a habit.

But today — something was different.

There, tucked between the armrest and the
wood, was a folded yellow note.
Soft corners. Clean fold. Like it hadn't been
lost...
Like it had been *placed.*

I should've ignored it.
Should've just looked away like I do with
most things now.
But something about it—
The stillness. The waiting.
It felt... familiar.

I picked it up. Slowly. Like it might disappear
if I moved too fast.
One glance at the handwriting — and my
world tilted.

Those soft curves.
The lowercase i with a circle instead of a
dot.
The uneven pressure on certain letters.

My hands went cold.
My pulse didn't.

"Maybe this is the only way I can talk to you
now.
I don't expect you to forgive me.
But I hope... one day, you'll read
everything."

– A

A.

Just one letter.
But it hit like a lifetime.

My breath caught somewhere between my
chest and the past.
This couldn't be happening.
Not now.

I looked around. Instinctively. Desperately.
Was this a joke?
Was someone watching me?

All I saw were strangers — walking dogs,
chasing toddlers, sipping chai.
No one who could've known.
No one who *should've* known.

I folded the letter again. Carefully. Like it might break.
My fingers trembled, but not from the cold.

Why now?
Why here?
Why *her*?

The name echoed in my head like a song I hated but couldn't skip.

Aarohi.

Two years.
Two long, bleeding years since she vanished.
No texts. No closure. Just silence.
And whispers behind my back from people who *thought* they knew.

"She moved on."
"She was with someone else."
"She cheated."

And I believed it.
Because believing the worst was easier than asking for the truth.
Truth hurts deeper.

But now this letter…
This soft echo of a voice I once knew better
than my own heartbeat.

"You didn't even say goodbye,"
I whispered under my breath.
"You just… disappeared."

I slipped the note into my pocket like it was
evidence of a ghost.
Got up. Walked away faster than usual.

But the wind felt colder now.
Like it carried the memory of something I
had buried too deep, too long ago.

I didn't look back at the bench.
I didn't need to.

Some part of me already knew —
This wasn't over.

And for the first time in years…
That scared me.

Chapter 2: The Cold Flame

*You don't notice when the warmth leaves
you.*
*But you feel it when someone tries to bring
it back.*

They say time heals.
That it softens the edges, makes memories
kinder.
But I don't think time heals anything.
It just teaches you how to carry pain with a
straight face.

And God, I had mastered that face.

Once, I used to be the guy people leaned
on.
Loud. Laughing. Making bad jokes at 3 a.m.
Now, even a casual "hi" feels like a question
I don't owe anyone answers to.

Most people think I'm arrogant.
Some call it attitude.

But the truth is simpler than that.
I'm just... tired.

Tired of pretending I'm fine.
Tired of being someone I no longer am.
Tired of dragging around the ruins of a
person I once loved... and maybe still do.

I kept the note in my drawer.
Didn't open it again.
Didn't need to.
It lived in my head now.
Every curve of that handwriting. Every
word.
Every silence it didn't fill.

A.
Aarohi.

The name stung like a paper cut. Small,
invisible... and always in the way.
I still remember the last time I saw her —
No drama. No goodbye. Just absence.

And then the whispers started.
That she was with someone else.
That I'd been nothing more than a stopover.

I didn't fight it.
I didn't ask.
Because if I asked... and she confirmed it...
I knew I wouldn't survive the answer.

But the part that hurt most?

She never denied it.
Never sent a message.
Never looked back.

And yet here I was, haunted by a single
letter.

Today, I walked into the library like usual.
Not for books.
For silence.

It was the only place I could breathe
without explanation.
No small talk. No forced smiles.
Just the comfort of corners and pages that
didn't ask questions.

I sat in my usual spot by the window.
Didn't expect anything.
Didn't want anything.

But fate's cruel. It sends you what you *don't* ask for.

Another note.
Same yellow paper.
Tucked into the pages of the book already waiting at my table.
I hadn't even checked it out.

My heart jumped before my hands did.

I unfolded it slowly.
Like I already knew what I'd find.

"I still remember the stories you told about stars.
You said they were dead... but still shining.
I wonder...
Are we like that too?"

No name.
No signature.
Just stardust and sadness pressed into words.

But only one person knew about that conversation.

Only one person had ever heard me say that.

Our last rooftop talk.
The night she looked at the stars like she was searching for something she couldn't keep.

Are we like that too?
Dead... but still shining?

I folded the letter again, slower this time.
My throat felt dry. My mind — louder than usual.

Is she here?
Watching me?
Leaving notes?

And if not her...
Then who?

Part of me wanted to crumple it.
Toss it into the nearest trash bin.

But I couldn't.
Because for the first time in two years...
Something inside me whispered—

What if you were wrong about her?

Chapter 3: Letters That Bleed (Part I)

You can bury memories under silence.
But they still bleed through the cracks.

By the time I found the third letter, I'd already stopped pretending I wasn't waiting for it.

It was late evening. College buzzed like usual — laughter echoing down corridors I no longer walked with friends, just passed through like a ghost with headphones. I never touched my locker anymore. There was nothing worth keeping in it. No books, no secrets.

But someone else had decided it was still worth opening.

And inside, quietly tucked in the corner like it belonged — was the third note.

Same paper. Same careful fold.
Same hand that once used to trace poems
on my palm with her fingertip.

I didn't even wait to be alone. I opened it
right there, in a corridor full of noise and
footsteps that didn't matter.

"Do you remember House No. 9?
The night it rained and we hid under that
broken tin shed?
You laughed so much that night... and I
laughed because of you."

House No. 9.

It hit me soft. No drama. No music swelling
in the background.

Just... her.

[Flashback – Two Years Ago]

It had started raining after that stupid
college party. We were half-drunk on soda
and laughter. She wore white — the color

she hated — only because once, casually, I'd said it looked good on her.

We ran through the streets like children, splashing through puddles, chasing each other through the chaos.

When the rain got heavier, she pulled me under a rusted tin shed beside an old broken house.

Aarohi (laughing, shivering):
"You owe me coffee. This is emotional damage. I'm wearing white in the rain, Raghav."
Me (grinning):
"You chose to wear it. That's self-inflicted pain."
Aarohi (nudging me):
"Liking you is self-inflicted too."

She said it like a joke.

I didn't laugh.
I just looked at her.
Really looked.

That was the moment.

I should've said something.
Anything.

But silence always feels safer than truth when you're afraid to lose what you already have.

[Back to Present]

I stared at the note for too long.

I could still smell the rain on her that night. Could still feel her hand brushing against mine under the shed. Could still hear my own heartbeat — loud and scared and stubborn.

And now this note.

After years of silence.
After I'd turned to stone so well, even I started to believe I couldn't feel anymore.

Why is she doing this?

Why now?

Why here?

I folded the letter gently and added it to the others.

Three letters.
And still, not a single explanation.
Only memories.

Memories that refused to stay buried.
Memories that bled — slow and quiet —
into everything I tried to forget.

I don't know what scared me more:
That it was her...
Or that it wasn't.

Because if someone else was writing these...
they knew too much.
They knew *us*.

And that's what terrified me.

Chapter 4: Letters That Bleed (Part II)

Sometimes, pain doesn't shout.
It leaves notes.

I didn't tell anyone about the letters.
Not because I wanted to protect her.
But because... I didn't know if she needed
protecting anymore.
And maybe — just maybe — I didn't want
the spell to break.

There was something hauntingly beautiful
about it — the way her voice slipped back
into my life, not through texts or calls or
second chances...

But through silence.

Through ink.

Through memories that refused to die
quietly.

Two days passed. I'd started watching shadows more closely. Checking behind me more than usual. My brain said it was nothing — coincidence, nostalgia, a prank maybe.

But my chest knew better.
It always does.

The fourth note came hidden inside a library book I hadn't even picked. The librarian just handed it over without looking. Some fiction novel with a worn-out spine. I flipped through it absentmindedly, pretending to read — until page 97.

There it was.

Folded, careful.

Like it didn't want to be found… but prayed to be seen.

"You weren't wrong to be angry.
You were wrong to never ask me why."

That line hit different.

It didn't burn like betrayal.
It didn't stab like memory.

It... *ached.*

It made me feel tired.

Tired of holding on to anger that had no proof.

Tired of running from a truth I never gave a chance to explain itself.

Tired of being the villain in a story I never understood.

I whispered to the page like it could hear me, like maybe she still could:

"Why didn't I ask? Why did I just... believe them?"

I told myself it was easier that way.
To hurt than to be hurt again.

But deep down?

I was scared.

Scared that her answer would break me in a way no rumor ever could.

[Flashback – One year before the silence]

We were under the banyan tree again —
our spot. Her head was in my lap. Her
fingers drawing tiny circles on my palm like
they were writing unsent letters.

Aarohi (softly):
"You trust too easily, Raghav."

Me (half-smiling):
"You say that like it's a bad thing."

Aarohi:
"It's not bad... it's beautiful.
But people like you...
you bleed faster."

Me (teasing):
"Then you better not be the one holding the
knife."

She didn't laugh. Just closed her eyes.

And now, two years later, I realize...
That silence of hers was the first goodbye.

[Back to Present]

Now, I can't even trust my own instincts.

Because someone is doing this — placing these notes with precision, like they know my routes, my routines, my ghosts.

Is it her?

Is it someone else?

Or is my mind finally breaking from the weight of everything I never dared to question?

Today in the library, I saw a girl sitting a few rows ahead. Rust-brown scarf. She kept looking over her shoulder, never directly at me, but never too far from line of sight either. She pulled a paper out of her bag. Same yellow edges. Same fold.

I froze.

I waited.

She left without a word.
And I didn't follow.

I just sat there, watching page 97,
whispering to myself like a man begging for
answers he's too afraid to hear:

**"If this is some kind of sick game… I'll end
it.
But if it's really you…
If it's really you, Aarohi…
Why now?"**

The question stayed unanswered.
Like all the others she left behind.

But one thing was clear now:

This wasn't over.
Not for me.
Not for her.
Not for *us* — whatever that still means

Chapter 5: Almost, Always

Some people don't leave.
They just vanish between the seconds you
weren't watching.

The days after the last letter felt like a
hollow performance.
I wore my body like borrowed skin.
I moved through lectures like a shadow
pretending to belong.
I smiled at people who didn't know I'd
stopped meaning it.

But beneath all that pretending—
I was still looking.

Benches.
Corners.
Library shelves.
Coffee sleeves.
Even the pocket of my hoodie, once—
as if hope could be folded small enough to
fit.

But hope doesn't knock twice.
It waits in silence.
Then disappears.

Until that fifth day.

It wasn't left for me this time.
It was dropped.

A whisper of paper on cold corridor floor.
A hand brushing past.
A figure turning the corner too quickly.
A soundless goodbye wrapped in ink.

I picked it up.
Didn't need to check.
I *knew.*

But this one was different.
It wasn't folded like the rest.
It was torn—
Edges wild, like it had been ripped from a storm.
Ink bleeding in places, like the words were crying.

"You think I chose to leave?"
"No, Raghav. I chose you. Every single time.
Even when it broke me."

And just like that—
my legs forgot how to move.
I froze in the middle of the hallway as the
world walked around me.
Someone bumped my shoulder.
Someone whispered.
Someone laughed.

But I just stood there.
Holding a scream between my teeth.
Because something inside me—
cracked.

**[Flashback – A Week Before She
Disappeared]**

Rain tapping like unanswered messages on
a windowpane.
She was late. Again.
I was angry. Again.
Over what?
I don't even remember anymore.

But I remember *my* voice.
And hers.

Me (sharply):
"It's always like this with you. Delay.
Confusion. Secrets."

Aarohi (softly):
"I was stuck with someone I couldn't avoid."

Me:
"Oh yeah? Who? That same guy everyone's
whispering about?"

Her face flickered.
Not anger.
Not guilt.
Just... disappointment.

Aarohi:
"You never even asked if it was true."
"You just... decided it was."

And then she left.
Hands shaking.
Eyes dimmed.

And I—
I let her go.

Because that day,
my ego was louder than her silence.

[Back to Present]

That night, I went back to the banyan tree.
The one where her head once rested on my
lap.
The one that knew the weight of her
laughter.

But this time,
it was just me.
And a torn letter that screamed what she
never did.

Me (a whisper):
"What happened to you, Aarohi?"
"Why didn't you shout back?"
"Why didn't you defend yourself?"

But the silence... stayed.
Still. Heavy.
Like a wound trying to heal without closure.

Except tonight, I didn't hate it.
I feared it.

Because it felt like something was slipping through.
Like time.
Like truth.
Like *her.*

And for the first time,
I wasn't looking for an apology.
Or closure.
Or even answers.

I was looking for forgiveness.

Not hers. *Mine.*

Chapter 6: What the Moon Heard

Some stories are never told out loud.
But the moon... she listens anyway.

It was waiting for me.
Not hidden.
Not slipped into a fold of shadow like the
others.
It was *there*—bold, fragile, unmissable—
taped dead-center on the faded notice
board outside the auditorium.

Like a dare.
Like a memory that refused to stay buried.

No one else stopped.
No one looked twice.
But I did.

Because by now, I could feel her
handwriting before I even saw it.
Like the tremble of a song you forgot you
once loved.

I pulled the note down.
Unfolded it with the kind of care you give to
something broken but beautiful.

And it read—

*"You once asked what I pray for when I see a
full moon."*
"I never answered."
*"I prayed you'd never look at me the way
you eventually did."*

I didn't breathe for a second.
Because I remembered.
I remembered that night too clearly.

[Flashback – 6 Months Before the Breakup]

Full moon.
Rooftop.
Her world tucked beneath her eyelids as she
made a silent wish to the sky.

Me (teasing):
"What are you praying for? Another coffee
date?"

Aarohi (eyes still shut):
"Peace."

Me (laughing):
"You already have me. What more peace do you want?"

She smiled.
But it wasn't her real one.
It was half a smile. The kind you wear when you're almost okay.

Aarohi (whispering):
"That's the thing, Raghav...
You make everything louder inside me."

I thought she meant love.
Intensity. Magic.
Maybe she did.

But maybe—
she also meant fear.

Because even then... I didn't fully trust her.
And love without trust is just a fear wearing perfume.

That night, she kept checking her phone.
Quick taps. Locked screen. Nervous fingers.

I'd laughed it off.

But something inside me whispered:
"Who's she hiding?"

That whisper never left.
It grew teeth.
It grew claws.
It fed on silence and bloomed into doubt.

[Back to Present]

I found myself on my building's rooftop
again.
Same sky. Same moon.
Only colder now.

Me (thinking):
"You prayed I'd never see you like that."
Doubting. Suspicious. Distant.
But I did.

I closed my eyes, like she had that night.
And for the first time...
I *prayed.*

Not for forgiveness.
Not for another chance.

But for *her*.

"If there's anything left of Aarohi in this
world...
let her know I was wrong."

Let her know I see now—
what I refused to back then.

Let her know the moon remembers.
Even if I tried to forget.

Chapter 7: In the Middle of Nowhere

Some answers don't come when you search for them.
They find you when you finally stop running.

It was one of those evenings—
Dusky. Soft-edged.
Where the light feels like it's been filtered
through memory.
And somehow, even the breeze feels
familiar.

I don't know why I was walking.
I wasn't trying to find anything.
Maybe I was just tired of staying still.
So I drifted... far from college, far from that
cursed bench, down a road I hadn't taken in
years.

It led to the old railway hill.
The place we only visited once.
One monsoon afternoon, skipping class,
soaked in rain and secrets.

[Flashback – That One Afternoon]

We sat beneath the crooked tin shelter,
our hands cold, our laughter warmer than
the tea we didn't buy.

Aarohi:
"You know what's scarier than dying?"

Me (grinning):
"Taxes?"

Aarohi (laughs softly):
"Being forgotten...
by someone who once said they couldn't
live without you."

She had smiled after saying it.
But it wasn't a joke.

Back then, I didn't realize how much of her
truth came disguised in laughter.

I reached the rusted bench on the edge of
the hill.
The metal was still cold—just like that day.

I sat down, resting my hands on my knees
like an old man carrying regrets instead of
bones.

That's when I saw it.

Wedged under the bench leg—
a thin, plastic folder.
Taped. Weathered. Waiting.

This wasn't coincidence anymore.
This was choreography.

I opened it with shaking fingers.

Not a letter this time.
No metaphors. No poetry.

Just a list.

"Things I gave up you never noticed —"
• My seat in the debate finals, because your
project needed finishing.
• A scholarship opportunity abroad,
because I didn't want to leave you behind.
• Weekends at home, because you were
scared to be alone during your dad's
hospital phase.
• My therapy appointments... because you

said people who needed help were weak.
• The truth — because I knew you wouldn't
believe it anyway.

My throat closed.

I read it again.

And again.

Me (thinking):
Wait. What truth?
What the hell did I not believe?

The list felt like a scream held in for too
long.
And every bullet point was a mirror I didn't
want to look into.

She'd been cutting herself out of her own
story—
just to let me be the hero in mine.

And I?
I called it *love*.

I stood up.
Pacing. Heart thudding.

I wasn't angry.
I was *wrecked.*

Because suddenly the silence I kept
craving...
it wasn't peaceful.

It was punishment.

Me (whispering):
"What if she never cheated?"
"What if she bled herself dry just to keep
me whole?"

I wanted to scream.
I wanted to tear the sky apart.
But all I did was fall back onto the bench
and bury my face in my hands.

And in a voice smaller than a whisper—

"Aarohi... where are you?"

No answer.
Not even from the wind.

Just the sound of a train passing far below.
Dragging behind it the years I wasted being
suspicious instead of *present.*

**[Flashback Insert – 3 Months Before She
Left]**

It was a lazy Saturday.
We sat on her rooftop with cold drinks and
soft clouds.

She was quiet.
Too quiet.

Me (lightly):
"You okay? Or is your soul buffering again?"

She chuckled faintly.
But her fingers tapped nervous patterns on
the chair's armrest.

Aarohi (gently):
"Have you ever felt like... you're not okay,
but not broken enough to ask for help?"

Me:
"C'mon. Everyone has down days. You just
need to distract yourself."

Aarohi (hesitating):
"What if distraction doesn't work? What if you... need actual help?"

I didn't hear it.
Not really.

Me (brushing it off):
"Yaar, people go to therapy these days for every little thing.
Just handle your own mess, right?"

I laughed.

She didn't.

She looked down. Bit her lip.
And whispered something I didn't even catch back then:

Aarohi (barely audible):
"Right..."

And that was the moment.
Right there.

The one where she started drowning—
and I mistook it for silence.

[Back to Present]

I stared at the list again.
My fingers trembling.
Not from cold.
From memory.

Me (thinking):
"You made her feel ashamed for needing
help."
"You laughed when she was trying to open
up."
"You assumed her silence was
manipulation, not a cry for mercy."

I folded the page slowly.
Like I was tucking away a piece of her I
never deserved.

I didn't know how many more truths were
buried in this trail.
But one thing had become brutally clear—

She didn't just leave me.
She left the version of herself she had to kill
to be with me.

She drowned quietly.
And I stood on the shore...
clapping,
thinking she was waving.

Chapter 8: Her Blog Was Her Blood

You think silence is absence... until you hear someone's truth in the places you never looked.

It was late.
Too late for sanity, too early for peace.

I hadn't slept.

The list from the hill wouldn't leave my mind.
Her sacrifices, her silences, her unsaid screams.
And the one haunting line I couldn't unsee:

"The truth — because I knew you wouldn't believe it anyway."

What truth?
What did I miss?

Or worse—
What did I kill before it could speak?

I needed answers.
But not the kind people give out loud.

The kind people bury.

So I went digital.

Logged into the only place I had never
thought to check:
Her blog.

Yeah. She had one.
Not public. Not promoted.
But once, long ago, she mentioned writing
somewhere "just for herself."

Back then I smiled and said,

"That's cute."

I never asked again.

I never cared to read.

And that—
That was my crime.

It took me hours.
Reddit threads. Forum scraps.
A forgotten username tucked in a year-old mail.

But I found it.

The blog.

Username: *she_writes_in_whispers*
Bio: "If I vanish, let my words be the evidence that I once existed."

My throat dried.

I clicked.

There weren't many posts.
Just **eight entries.**
No titles. Just dates.
Spread across two years—
Each one felt like a timebomb.

I clicked the first.

Entry: 03 June, 2018

He makes me laugh so easily.
And yet, I wonder if he'd notice when I'm
crying behind the same smile.
Today he said he loved me for being so
strong.
And all I could think was—strength
shouldn't be measured by how well you
pretend to be okay.

I stared.
Re-read.
And kept going.

Entry: 17 Sept, 2018

Sometimes I want to scream.
Tell him that being with someone who sees
you as "emotionally sorted" is the loneliest
feeling in the world.
I wish he'd ask twice when I say I'm fine.
I wish I didn't have to break just to be
believed.

Entry: 29 Jan, 2019

He thinks I'm overreacting.
But how do you explain trauma to someone
who sees the world in black-and-white?
I saw something today—something I
couldn't unsee. It shook me. I tried to tell
him.
But he just said, "You're being paranoid."
So I swallowed it. Like always.
Maybe one day I'll choke.

I scrolled, faster now.
Like each post was a shard of glass I *needed*
to bleed on.

And then—

Entry: 07 Nov 2019
Just weeks before she disappeared.

Entry: 07 Nov, 2019

He thinks I betrayed him.
But what he doesn't know is—
I was trying to protect him from something

I sat back.

The screen blurred.

Something inside me collapsed quietly—
not with sound,
but with *weight*.

I had built this whole damn narrative.
Painted her with colors I *chose*.

Never realizing she was bleeding in hues I
refused to see.

The girl I loved...
wasn't just hurting.

She was *hiding*.

And not from the world—
but from **me.**

I scrolled to the last post.

There was no text.
Just an image.

A painting.

Drawn by her.
Black and white.
A silhouette of a girl—half fading, half
screaming.

Captioned:

"If I disappear, remember: I tried to stay."

That was it.

No goodbye.
No finale.
Just echoes.

And suddenly, every word she ever said to
me played back—
but in reverse.
And this time,
I heard them.

Me (barely breathing):
I made her feel like the villain...
...when all she wanted was to be saved.

Chapter 9: Echoes Between the Pages
Sometimes, finding someone isn't about chasing — it's about listening where they last spoke.

Two days.
That's how long I spent with her voice folded between my fingers.
Reading.
Rereading.
Forgetting to breathe.
Remembering how it felt to be seen and still not understand.

Sleep didn't visit.
Food didn't matter.
And the world outside blurred like fog on glass.

Grief is a strange language.
It doesn't scream.
It *settles*.
Quietly.

Like dust on a book you should've read
when it still mattered.

But grief alone isn't movement.
It's a weight.
And I needed wings.

So I walked back into a place I thought I had
locked behind me —
The college library.
Same walls. Same stillness.
But nothing felt the same.

I hadn't stepped in here since everything fell
apart.
It smelled of old ink and fresher lives.
A silence too perfect to belong to the
broken.

I wandered.
Up the staircase that creaked like time
remembering.
Second floor.
Far left corner.
Her favorite place.

She used to sit there —
Near the window that poured light like

forgiveness.
Sketching. Scribbling.
That little green notebook with the crescent
moon sticker always in her lap.
Aarohi didn't just read books.
She *spoke* to them.

I sat there now.
Alone.
Listening.

And the chair answered.
Not with creaks.
But with a whisper folded into paper.

A torn page —
barely tucked between the backrest and
cushion.
Like a secret trying to breathe.

I pulled it out.
And just like that, she was speaking again.

Aarohi's handwriting
*You're probably not reading this, but if by
chance you are...*

I hope the words feel familiar.
Because that's all I ever wanted — for you
to see the parts of me you always looked
through.

I didn't leave to punish you.
I left because staying meant disappearing
piece by piece.
And I was already almost gone.

My fingers clenched around the page.

Raghav (internal)
Why do her words feel like glue now...
when back then I treated them like static?

She wasn't just writing notes.
She was breathing pieces of herself into
places we once shared.

The bench on the hill.
This corner of the library.

Each message wasn't random.
They were echoes.

And echoes don't just happen.
They follow sound.
They follow *voice*.

A trail.

Raghav (internal)
If there's a trail...
there's a destination.

I stood up.
For the first time in days — no, months —
with something like purpose burning
beneath my ribs.

This wasn't mourning anymore.
This was motion.
A slow unraveling of silence she left behind.

She didn't want me to chase her.
She wanted me to *understand* her.

And I was finally — painfully — starting to
listen.

Chapter 10: A Voice in the Dust

Some trails aren't marked on maps. They're hidden in moments we didn't care to notice before.

It wasn't just a note anymore.
It was a pattern.
A map drawn in silence.

The bench.
The library.
Each place Aarohi chose wasn't random —
it was *hers*.
A fingerprint of emotion pressed into
forgotten corners.
And now I remembered another.

An old memory flickered —
a time I followed her after a fight.
She thought I'd left.
But I watched from across the street as she
disappeared into a quiet art supply shop
behind the railway colony.

She didn't go there to buy.
She went there to *breathe* —
to be alone but still surrounded by color.
Aarohi's form of survival.

I never asked why.
I just walked away.

But today... I walked in.

6:47 PM
The door creaked open, the bell above it
letting out a tired chime.
The place smelled of paint thinner and old
dreams.

Dried brushes leaned like wilted flowers in
metal cans.
Sketchbooks were stacked like unread
memories.
A silence lived here — not heavy, not
hollow... just honest.

Behind the counter sat an old woman with
silver strands coiled into a messy bun.

She looked up from a crossword puzzle as I
stepped closer.

Raghav:
"Hi… um, sorry to bother. Do you remember
a girl who used to come here often?
Big sketchbook… green hoodie sometimes…
moon sticker on her bag?"

Her eyes didn't blink — they studied.
Like she wasn't looking *at* me,
but *through* me.
Through the years I had let slip by.

Shopkeeper:
"You mean Aarohi?"

The name hit like a skipped heartbeat.
Sharp. Sudden. Familiar in a way that hurt.

Raghav:
"Yes… do you know where she is?"

She didn't answer right away.
Just reached below the counter —
slow, deliberate.

And pulled out a yellowed envelope.
My name on it.
Her handwriting.

To Raghav — in case you ever show up.

The air in the room froze.
Like time was waiting for me to catch up.

I opened it slowly.
As if the paper might shatter in my hands.

Inside was a painting —
thick watercolor paper.
Faded around the edges, but deliberate.

A bench on a hill.
A girl with headphones, her back to the
world, hair catching the wind.

Below it, in small inked letters:

You never really looked.

That's when it hit me.
She wasn't painting to decorate.
She was painting to *speak*.

Every stroke — a syllable.
Every color — a memory I failed to hold.

This wasn't art.
This was language.
Her language.

And I?
I'd never learned to read it.
Not until she stopped speaking it.

Raghav (internal):
This isn't a search anymore.
It's a conversation I never let her finish.

I stepped out into the dusk.
The painting pressed against my chest like a
heartbeat I almost forgot I had.

The sky was folding into night.
But for the first time,
I wasn't walking into darkness.

I knew where to go next.
Not where *she* would be —
but where *we* used to be.

A place not hers.
Not mine.

Ours.

Chapter 11: Where Silence Spoke First

Some places remember more than people do.

It was rusted now.
The old railway bridge.
The kind of place that didn't belong in postcards —
but it belonged to *us*.

No one else ever knew about it.
Hidden just outside town, past a cluster of eucalyptus trees and forgotten tracks.
We used to climb the side railings, legs dangling above the quiet earth,
pretending that a passing train could carry our sadness away.

It wasn't beautiful.
But it was *ours*.
Raw. Quiet. Honest.

The last time we were here...
was her birthday.

I had given her a handmade keychain with
her initials.
She gave me a letter — folded with care,
wrapped in nervous hope.
I told her I'd read it later.
I never did.

I didn't realize that silence could sound like
betrayal too.

The bridge creaked beneath my steps.
The metal cold against my palms as I
gripped the railing and sat —
same spot as always.
My shadow stretched beside me, but I
imagined *her* there instead.
Feet swinging. Hair dancing in the wind.
Humming that off-key tune she only sang
when she was thinking.

Raghav (internal):
Why didn't I come here sooner?

Maybe because I didn't want the place to tell me the truth.

But it did.

As my fingers grazed beneath the beam,
they brushed against something —
small, plastic, taped to the underside.

A ziplock pouch.
Worn by time.
Hidden like a secret only meant to be found
by someone who finally cared enough to look.

Inside?

Aarohi's **green notebook**.

My hands trembled as I opened it.
The pages smelled like her —
like old paper, rain, and unspoken thoughts.

First page:
"This isn't a diary. It's a voice. The one I could never raise loud enough for you to hear."

Every page after that was a wound.
Unsent letters.
Half-drawn sketches.
Thoughts crossed out, rewritten, re-felt.

She had poured herself into silence.
Because I never gave her space to speak aloud.

Aarohi (written):
"You once told me I never talk about my feelings.
But when I did, you didn't listen.
You judged."

"So I stopped trying."

One page near the end was folded.
Pressed tighter than the rest.

I unfolded it.
And there it was.

Aarohi's Note:
"If you're reading this, you finally came back here.
That means something.

Maybe you miss me.
Maybe you're sorry.
Maybe you still don't understand."

"But Raghav...
I didn't cheat on you.
I loved you.
I just got tired of proving it."

"– A"

The notebook slipped from my hands and
fell into my lap.
The wind roared around me —
but inside, everything was still.

Still...
and shattered.

Raghav (internal):
I made her invisible.
Doubted her love.
Twisted her silence into guilt.
And then used it to walk away.

All this time,
I thought she broke me.

But the truth?
I broke myself.

Because I never listened to the voice I never
heard.

Chapter 12: The Voice I Never Heard

Regret is never loud. It whispers — when no one's left to hear it.

I didn't sleep that night.
Couldn't.
Aarohi's notebook lay beside me like a
fragile heartbeat —
each page a moment I had missed,
each word a mirror I couldn't escape.

I had her voice now.
But not her.

Still, something in me had changed.
A slow cracking of the shell I had buried
myself in for too long.
Grief had turned to clarity.
And clarity demanded I do something.

I had to find her.
Not for answers.
Not for closure.

But to say the one thing I never said when it mattered.

I'm sorry.

I reached out to everyone I could think of —
college friends, hostel mates, random
connections I barely remembered.
Most were blanks. Some were echoes.

"She left after college."
"Deleted her socials."
"Changed her number."
"No one really knew where she went."

It was like chasing fog.
Every lead slipped through my fingers.

Until one late evening,
a message pinged back.

Her old roommate.
We hadn't spoken in years.

"Last I heard... she moved to Shimla. Art
residency. Quiet little retreat in the hills. But
that was months ago."

Shimla.

Of course.

She once told me,
"I want to live in the hills one day — where even the silence feels like poetry."

I packed that night.
Didn't think. Didn't plan.
Just moved.

Two trains. A bus. A walk through winding pine-scented roads.

And suddenly, I was standing outside a quiet art retreat halfway up a mountain.
Paintings lined the porch like memories left out to dry.
The wind whispered like her —
soft, sad, and gone.

A man stood by the gate. Older. Kind eyes.

Caretaker:
"Yes?"

Raghav:

"I'm looking for… Aarohi."

He studied me, like my face was a question
he half-remembered.

Caretaker (quietly):

"You just missed her."

The words hit harder than I expected.
Like missing a heartbeat.
Or waking up from a dream too late.

Caretaker:

"She left a few weeks ago. Said she was
done waiting for people to come find her."

My throat burned.

Caretaker (softly):

"But she left something behind."

He reached into a small drawer behind him.
Pulled out a letter.
My name on the front. Her handwriting.

Again.

To Raghav.

I opened it like it might break.
Inside:

Aarohi's Final Note:
*"Maybe one day you'll understand that I
didn't leave because I wanted to.
I left because I needed to heal."*

*"If you're reading this... please don't search
anymore."*

"Live. Write. Love better."

*"That's all I ever wanted — for you to hear
me."*

"This was my voice."
"– A"

And just like that,
it was over.

Not with a goodbye.
But with a truth.

I stood there for a long time,
letter trembling in my hands,
the silence heavier than ever.

Because I had heard her now.
But she was gone.

And maybe she wouldn't come back.
Maybe this was the last page.

But it wasn't the end of the story.

Because somewhere between all the notes
she left,
all the silences I finally listened to,
I found something I had never looked for.

Her.

The real her.

And maybe…
in those pages…
I was starting to find myself too.

Epilogue: The Last Page
*Some stories don't need closure. They just
need to be remembered.*

I never wrote this book to find her.

I wrote it because... after everything —
every silence, every missed moment, every
unread word —
I finally heard her.

Not just the letters.
Not just the lines in a hidden notebook.

But the pauses between her sentences.
The way she looked away when she wanted
me to listen.
The way she stayed — even when it hurt.

At every book fair, someone always asks:

"Is it real?"
"Was she real?"
"Did you ever find her again?"

I smile.
A little too long.
A little too sadly.

And say:
**"Some stories don't need a reunion.
They just need a reader."**

The last time I visited the hilltop bench, it
had changed.

New names carved into the wood —
new love, new stories.

But in the corner, still clinging on...

"R + A"

Faded.
But not gone.

Much like her.

I sat there for hours,
her notebook in my lap,
the breeze flipping pages like a ghost
reading over my shoulder.

And I realized —

Maybe one day,
she'll walk into a quiet bookstore,
run her fingers across this cover,
whisper the title like a memory:

The Voice I Never Heard.

And she'll know.

That I finally listened.
That every page was for her.
That I never stopped waiting.

Because the voice I couldn't hear back then
echoes in me now —
in every silence I carry,
in every word I write.

The Voice I Never Heard
was never just hers.

It became mine too.

And maybe...

Just maybe...

This wasn't the last page after all.

A Note from the Author

Some stories don't begin as stories. They begin with a silence, a moment that lingers, or a feeling that never quite leaves. This one wasn't something I planned to write. It came from something personal—something I couldn't say out loud, so I let the pages speak for me.

I didn't write this to be a novel. I wrote it to process what I couldn't explain. Sometimes, when someone leaves without giving you answers, the only way to understand is to write your way through the questions.

People often ask if this story is real. If the characters existed. If I ever found the person I was writing about. I don't usually give a straight answer—because maybe the truth is somewhere in between.

But if something in this story felt familiar to you—if it reminded you of someone, or made you feel something you thought you had forgotten—then maybe, you already have the answer.

Thank you for reading *The Voice I Never Heard*.
And for listening closely.

— Vasudev Rathva

About the Author

Vasudev Rathva is a storyteller who listens to the silences people leave behind. Known for his emotionally intense and poetic narratives, he writes not just to tell a story—but to echo the unheard voices within us all. His writing bridges the worlds of emotion and mystery, often capturing the ache of unspoken love, the weight of misunderstood moments, and the beauty of lingering hope.

By day, Vasudev is immersed in the technical and business world, but by night, he finds his truest expression in ink and imagination. He believes that stories don't always need loud drama—sometimes the softest heartbreak leaves the deepest scars. With a style that blends realism, lyrical introspection, and suspense, his goal is to make readers feel every breath of his characters' journeys.

The Voice I Never Heard is his debut novel—a soul-stirring exploration of love, loss, and the emotional ruins we often build within ourselves. Through this story, Vasudev invites you into a world where silence speaks louder than words, and where every letter written from the heart carries a truth too powerful to ignore.

Thank You !

9 798899 062322